His death was the beginning of a long journey

Robert G Wright

Copyright © 2010 Author Name

All rights reserved.

ISBN:1461081289
ISBN-13:9781461081289

DEDICATION

This story is dedicated to the great people of Claryville, MO and the brave soldiers that I served with in Vietnam and a friend that we helped each other find our way home.

CONTENTS

	To beloved Mary Pauline Gibbar	I
1	Death was the beginning	1
2	Jacob Gibbar	13
3	Mary Pauline	41
4	Mary and Jacob become man and wife	46
5	Some time alone	58
6	The first year	63
7	Now they are five	65
8	Jacob leaves one more time	69
9	The unwilling host	74
10	Together they find their way home	112

ACKNOWLEDGMENTS

To my wife Jane Emily (Favier) Wright that made this book possible and to the people of Perryville, Mo that shared their knowledge of the bottoms that allowed this story to be told.

1 DEATH WAS THE BEGINNING

His death was not by hostile fire, as his lifeless body lay in a far remote country called Vietnam. Maybe it would be recorded as an accident or by hostile fire. But this would not alter the fact or bring comfort to the love ones left back at home. As life fading and the world that he once knew grew dark. He felt that somehow he found peace in this land so far away from home. It was like a new birth, for the first time in his life, he felt no pain, no fear, and the earthly laws that bound us to our mortal existence seemed to no longer exist. He felt free and towards the heavens a light shone down as if to guide him as many lighthouses have guided ships to a safe passage. His curiosity was over whelmed and, he floating towards the light as a moth to a candle. He heard the men under his charge calling his name, at first, it went unnoticed, but they were persistent until it could no longer be ignored. His trip towards the light came to a halt as he turned toward the voices.

The morning started out normal, hot, humid and looking forward to a trip to the mess hall for something they called food. It would be a few hours before it was time to be deployed. It gave us time to clean weapons, and stock up on supplies then plan out the nighttime operation. If there was any time left, write a letter home and tell them how safe and sound you were. These letters were mostly lies; you always felt that maybe the next time in the field, death had you on his list to be claimed. The lies in the letters, maybe the love one's back home would believe but more than likely they knew you were hiding the truth. It was the time of the month when the squad was deployed to perform a joint operation with the Navy. As the day grew into darkness, our trip down the Mekong River began, when the radar on the swift boat found a promising location we would be drop off to set up an ambush. A man on the bow used a starlight scope to try and avoid being ambushed. The scope was design to amplify the light from the moon but for the most part it displayed a hazy green world and a false sense of security. This trip would be a little more trying than most, a trial under fire for three soldiers that just arrived in country. It would take a few trips in the field before a trust could be built between them and the rest of the squad. Over come with fear they might start shooting at anything that moved including the rest of the squad. A Navy Swift boat transported us down the River, these trips always felt like a life time. Too much time to think, remembering the friends that have falling, ones that lived and the ones that died. Always having fear of making new friends just to see them die, Will I be next or see another day. Please God let us all go home. We were dropped on the riverbank, on one side a rice paddy and the river at our backs. We set up as we did a countless time before. Side by side with a few feet between us, staring into the darkness and straining to hear any type of sound. I heard my name whispered and started to towards the voice. The patch of land that we sat upon was about six feet off the water, and very narrow. Before I could reach the source of the voice a blunt object struck the back of my neck, I fell face first into the rice paddy and was unconscious

As I walk among living I feel sadness

I have died twice and no long feel that I fit

The living will one-day will find their just reward in the heavens above

But for those who are damned but pure of heart will find no such reward

We will walk among the living and try and make up for the wrongs that we have committed

Just a few hours prior I made a promise, I gave my word, to bring the men under my charge back safe and alive. The light from above also made the earth beneath as bright

His death was the beginning of a long journey

as day. A body laying face down in the water caught my attention. A fear was struck, one of the men had been lost, and another friend had died. Floating beneath the body, it was a face seen countless times before in a mirror.

The eyes were lifeless; it appeared that he gasp for the last breath air that was no longer within his reach. Somewhere in the darkness he screamed a silent scream and the next moment he and his body were one. The pain was greater than he ever experienced before, he expelled from his lungs what felt like the contents of an ocean. Once he was on solid land he laid half in shock and totally confused. It would be a few more days before the full impact of the experience would be comprehended. At first fear set in, then grief, he wished that he had continued the journey toward the light instead of to his body. This wonderment of the light would haunt him the rest of his life. Also, the fear of sharing his near death experience grew as the days of his life passed. As he watched his love ones grow old and on the thresh hold of death. He was afraid to share with them not to fear death because death is not the end but the beginning of a new life without pain, without worry, an experience that cannot be described by mere words.

His death was the beginning of a long journey

JACOB GIBBAR

That brief moment that his body laded in the water lifeless and before his soul and body could become one, a much weaker life force entered. The weaker life force was a man that died many years prior. His name was Jacob Clements Gibbar; Jacob birthplace was in a small farming community in a place that no longer existed. A small town called Claryville, Missouri. The town in its haw-day barely saw a population over hundred people; the eastern portions of the town were against and part of the levy that kept the mighty Mississippi River in its place. This is also where the ferry was located that ran between Claryville and Chester Illinois. Chester was a much larger city than Claryville and to most it was the big city, full of lights and fancy stores. The population of Chester was around 1,000 residences. The area that Claryville was located in was called the bottoms, in the spring the snows from further up north would melt, and sometimes causing the river to over flow its banks and the bottoms and the river would become one. This was before the levees were built which gave everyone a false sense of security. To the Far West, in the distance the land rose and formed a long ridge that seemed to stretch to the sky despite its size, it would later be referred to as McBride hill. In the past when the river would overflow it banks the ridge became the new bank of the river. On top of the ridge was a city called Perryville. The soil that composed the bottoms was very rich and fertile and was made for farming. The town itself had a few houses, a hotel for the weary travelers, a bank, a very small church and a general store that was very small and carried just the bare necessities. The main population of Claryville lived in the farms that lay on the out skirts of the town.

The fall of 1915 is when Jacob decided not to follow in the steps of his father as a sharecropper. Jacob father's Jacob Senior always had a very difficult time raising a family and having food on the table and cloths on their backs. His plot of land was close to 100-acres, it had a barn that had seen better days a small house and way too many mouths to feed. Jacob senior had the use of the land, after the harvest and the crops were sold; half of the profit went to the owner of the land. Some years when

His death was the beginning of a long journey

money was tight Jacob senior was force to purchase seed and supplies on credit. The general store took a big risk extending credit and after a couple of farms failed owing a good sum of money, the store was force to charge fifth teen per interest to remain open. Some years when the rains failed and the hot summer days took their tolls, Jacob senior could not break even, if it weren't for his wife's garden, raising chickens for eggs and canning, the family during these lean times wouldn't have food on the table. Jacob's mother name was Colleena, she was always busy, if she wasn't cooking, tending the chickens or her garden, she was patching cloths to make them last a little while longer or letting them out or taking them in for hand me downs for a younger brother or sister. In the winter months after the growing season ended they would set down and count their blessing or lack of blessing. For the most part it was the latter. The wintertime was a time for hunting and most times the menu in the household was rabbit. Sometimes a deer was added but that was rare.

It was during these hard times that Jacob felt that if there were one less month to feed than the family would be better off. A few of his friends found work on the packet boats that was always busy hauling produce to the south, goods to the north. The packet boats at that time were the way people traveled to different parts of the country. The river at times had a little over a thousand packet boats operating. It was the only way to travel, but within ten years rail travel would cause the end of this mode of transportation. Rail travel was faster and safer, and reached many cities that were not along the riverbanks.

When a packet boat landed, Jacob would seek out the captain of the boat to secure a job. Jacob was turned away countless times, life was hard on these vessels and many young men would jump ship after the first payday and head for home. It was tiresome spending a few weeks training someone just to have them find the work too difficult and disappear at the first port with their first month's paycheck. Jacob was finding it almost hopeless when he met a man they called Captain Jack his packet boat was called the Saint Mary. Nervously he approached him and let him know he was trying to find work on the river. Jacob said he would work for free and if Captain Jack did not like his work he could be drop off at one of the many ports along the river.

Captain Jack looked into Jacob's eyes for the longest time, he seen something that reminded him of himself when he was that age. He stood up and said "son we have a deal, can you be ready to go in one hour". Jacob was speechless and only managed to say "yes sir and thank you" a couple of times. Jacob ran home and threw his belongings in a gunnysack and ran back to the river dock. He was excited and relieved that the Saint Mary was still docked and the job offer was not just a way for Captain Jack to rid himself of someone that would not take no for an answer.

Captain Jack instructed his crew that a new man was joining and to work him hard and long. "He's working for free and if he last a month then we will talk about pay".

True to Captain Jack word, Jacob the first couple of weeks received very little sleep. At times he was throwing coal in the furnace to produce steam for the engines, lashing down cargo when fierce storms threaten to wash them over board. The cook also found work for Jacob peeling potatoes and washing dishes. Jacob never complained his thoughts would travel back to Claryville and to a young lady. Jacob's heart belonged to this young woman in Claryville. Her name was Mary Pauline Schroeder. Mary's hair was almost black, her eyes were blue and when she became upset they turned green, she was small but very wiry. Mary had a heart of gold and a very hot temper, in her younger days many young people in Claryville found that when she became upset her fists would start flying. Mary was a strong person, she always spoke her mind but she was also very gentle with animals. Every Sunday at Claryville church Mary would always find a place to set in the front pew, her hand me down clothes might have been a little worn and faded, but she look like a little angel that came down from heaven. She had a smile and a little twinkle in her blue eyes that would melt a person heart.

After a few weeks, the crew looked upon Jacob as a good person and one that would last, they worked him almost around the clock and he never complained. He would always complete what every task he was given and look forward to the next. One afternoon Captain Jack called him up to his cabin, Jacob was nerves, his thoughts turned into questions "did I do something wrong". By the time Jacob reaches the cabin door he was ready to receive some bad news. He would find some way to make it back to the only place that he could call home. As he entered the cabin, Captain Jack was busy with paperwork and asked Jacob to take a seat. After what seemed like a lifetime, he laid his wooden pen down, and looked Jacob in the eyes. "Remember our deal, if you didn't work out, you would work for free and I could drop you off at the next port" He went on to say "I kind of knew" and he was interrupted by a knock on the door.

It was a crewmember informing him that they would be docking in about twenty minutes. Called to Captain's cabin, landing in twenty minutes, what did I do wrong Jacob thought? He tried to apologize and the Captain just laughed "now Jacob let me talk, we had a deal that you would work for free and if you didn't work out I could drop you off at the next port". Jacob looked down at his feet wait for the worse. There was a long pause and Captain Jack said "son I had a feeling about you, you reminded me of my younger days. I would be proud if you would join my crew and yes you been on the payroll the day you started" Jacob thank him many times, and as he walked out on to the deck he had a very broad smile on his face, thinking Mary our dreams will come true.

Jacob days became a lot simpler, he was now a member of the crew and worked the normal crew hours, six hours on and six hours off. The older crewmembers took him under their wings and started teaching him everything that needed to be known to run the Saint Mary. Jacob spent a few days in the engine room and Everett who was the engineer explained how the boiler and the steam engine worked. Everett commented it was one of the greatest things ever invented; it could be one of your best friends or your worst enemy. He went on to

His death was the beginning of a long journey

explain, if the boiler becomes clogged and blows up it would sink the Saint Mary and more than likely take everyone with it. Everett started talking about the past, "when I was your age it took us about a month to go from ST Louis to New Orleans the boat were nothing like they are today". "They were made out of logs and we had to use long poles to travel down the river, there was no engines" due to the movement of the river, it was impossible to bring them back" He went on to explain the cargo would be unloaded and the log boat sold off for the wood. The trip back was by horse and wagon, and then it would start all over again. .

The trip from Claryville to New Orleans only took a few weeks. The largest town Jacob every visited up to that point was Chester. Later that evening a couple of the crewmembers invited Jacob to tag along; he found it to be a different world. He blushed when a lady of the evening whispered something in his ear. His friends just laughed and patted him on his back, Jacob commented that he would see them later, and made a hasty retreat. Jacob found his way back to the Packet boat, and thought to himself that there only one woman for me and he made a promise "Mary I will stay true". Jacob did return the next morning and visited a couple of shops. He picked up a present for Mary and came across a pouch made out of something called rubber that a man could carry his wallet in and keep it dry.

After his little visit to New Orleans that most people called Sin City, at other ports he would spend his off time on the packet boat. The boat had a few books to read and an old deck of playing cards, it helped the time past until the cargo was loaded and packet boat was on its way.

Jacob over the months learned everything that he could about this vessel that would one-day make Mary and his dreams come true. Every few months the Saint Mary would dock at Claryville, Jacob would be on the bow measuring the depth of the water, sand bars were always disappearing just to reappear at another location. Between measurements, he would look closely at the landing for Mary. Mary always had a stump she would set on when she completed her chores. After the Saint Mary docked they had a chance to speak for a few minutes then Jacob would be busy for most of the daylight hours unloading and loading cargo. The packet boat would stay docked until early the next morning. Mary and Jacob would spend that time just being together talking and telling stories.

The next morning they would again say their farewells and try to make it through the rest of the day without sleep. The trip north was just for a few days, a stop in St Louis then the might packet boat would turn around and head south.

Jacob's stop on this trip would be across the river in Chester and was always close to twelve o'clock noon when it arrived. Early in the morning Mary would pack a picnic lunch and ride the ferry across to Chester to meet Jacob. This stop would only be a few hours, Captain Jack and the crew would fill in for Jacob for about an hour so he could spend time with Mary. The hour would pass by swiftly and the packet boat steam whistle would toot two shorts to let Jacob know it was time to leave. The time passed slowly and only in their dreams would they be together. Jacob and Mary would look into each other's eyes and knew that one day they would be together till the end of time. For Jacob when he pulled his shift, he had a very little time to think of Mary, it was the hours meant for rest and sleep that would haunt his dreams. He would see her in his dreams, her black hair and blue eyes and her angelic smile.

Some times while traveling the river a rowboat would tie up to the packet boat when it was docked. It was always late in the afternoon, when the packet boat was waiting for first light to continue the trip. These ladies for a small sum of money would fulfill a man's dream. They had many names but Jacob would always remember them by the ladies of the night or some called them nighthawks. When these ladies descended, Jacob would find some quite place, he knew that if had falling victim to the temptation of the flesh he would never be able to look Mary in the eyes again.

His death was the beginning of a long journey

Jacob when he was young, some mornings he would spend it in the kitchen with his mother Colleena, helping her preparing the foods that composed the family meals during the day. Jacob always enjoyed making bread; his mother taught him the receipt that was taught to her by her mother in Germany. The receipt was never writing down, it was something that was etched in their minds.

Jacob found refuge in the galley, away from the nighthawks making bread, which lasted long enough for the temptation to leave. For the next few days the cook and crew dined on bread that they said must have been sent down from heaven. The cook was always trying to duplicate the receipt but she always failed. Jacob out of habit would add the ingredients by memory, a pinch of this a hand full of that. It would have been an art that would have been lost in time by future generation. Jacob in the far future would make it a present to a friend that helped him find his way home and to find Mary.

The packet boat kept Jacob busy, and he was assigned many tasked. Captain Jack on some days had Jacob fill out the logs for the cargo being transported to various ports. On Sunday morning Jacob would always report to the galley to make Colleena's bread that the cook just couldn't master. Jacob could find life on the river enjoyable if his heart didn't ache for Mary. The packet boat was a little under three hundred feet in length and required daily maintenance due overloaded cargo that at times threaten to sink it. It seem like every few months the boiler would show it age, and the next few days was spent anchored in the middle of the river. Everett would be below deck and it sounded like he was beating the boiler to death, using every word he could find and some new ones that were never heard on the river and probably not on this planet. Jacob and the rest of the crew would spend the time painting what needed to be painted and scraping barnacles off the sides of the Saint Mary. After a while smoke would start escaping from the smokestack and everyone knew in about an hour the boilers were made ready and the paddle wheels would come to life. It was a rush to store the cans of paint, cleaning paintbrushes and to load the small boat back on the packet boat that was used by a crewmember scraping barnacles. When Everett had the boiler up to full steam no force on this earth could stop the Saint Mary from continuing her journey. Everett would always say "time is money, and this is cutting

His death was the beginning of a long journey

into my money". The Saint Mary was the pride of the river; it was one of the few steam powered packet boats that if it did well then each crewmember would receive a bonus. This was unheard of during this time period but Captain Jack felt if a person gave all they could then they should be rewarded.

Jacob would keep his pay in the rubber pouch he purchased in New Orleans, in Captain Jack safe. Every few months they would have a layover in Claryville or Chester and Jacob would deposit his and Mary future in the bank of Claryville. The people working in the bank knew that Jacob and Mary would become man and wife one day but they kept it a secret that they both had separate accounts in the bank. As the bank president once commented "when they are ready to tell each other they will".

On one cold winter day, it was close to freezing when the packet boat made it stop in Claryville, there were a couple inches of snow and the wind was very brisk coming from the North. Mary was setting on the stump shivering and reading a book. Jacob became very upset. He scolded Mary for being out in the cold, "if you became sick and died I would not have any reason to live". "Mary one day we will have enough saved up to start our home, we will be together for so long you might grow tired of me" Mary had a smirk on her face, then she smiled and they both start laughing. "If I ever get tired of you Jacob Clements Gibbar, I will just throw you back in the river where I found you" Mary said. Jacob had a few hours of handling cargo before he could spend time with Mary. Jacob ask her to wait in the general store until he could join her and he commented "You owe me a cup of coffee for all the grief you put me through, waiting out here in the cold". Mary walked to the general store and every once in a while she would walk out to see if the cargo transfer was complete. Half the time Jacob would spot her and wave his arms to get her back into the store. This went on for a few hours before Jacob was able to join her. Jacob looked into Mary's eyes and said "Mary I asked you to wait in the store and what do you do, keep running out in the middle of town looking towards the river. I had to wave you back in. what am I going to do with you" Mary just smiled and held up her left hand and started counting". "One: we can spend the rest of our lives together, two you can let me give you my heart, and three you can give me your heart to keep me company when you are gone". "Four we can love each other forever". "Five" Mary paused and repeated five a couple more times. Jacob smiled and said " well Mary what about number five" Mary just laugh, and commented "Jacob Gibbar the second after we are Married if you ever leave me again, remember the first time we met in Sunday school. You ended up in the corner setting on a stool after I give you a shiner, that will seem like a holiday compared to next time" Mary's eyes turn green and they both laughed and hugged for the longest time. Then tears grace both their eyes, the warmth they felt from each other, the love that they shared, the desire to start their lives together would have to be put on hold for a little longer. They sat and shared a few cups of coffee together, filling each other in on each other lives.

They were planning as they did in the past, spend the night talking to each other when they heard the Saint Mary's two short toots on the steam whistle. Jacob jump up and said "something is wrong" they ran down to the landing.

Captain Jack express his sorry for such a short visit but the river was icing over and they had to turn the packet boat south before it was stuck. It was a hard trip for the boat and crew; the packet boat had to travel slowly. The crew took turns on the bow of the ship with long poles pushing the large chunks of ice out of the way that could pierce the hull and send everyone to their death in an ice grave". After forty-eight hours the packet boat was in warmer water and safe from the ice. That year 1917 the northern states suffer an extremely cold winter, many of the packet boats were stuck in the ice waiting for spring thaw. Captain Jack packet boat was safe down river, but the routes that he built delivering cargo up north were out of reach do to the ice. The packet boat made it to New Orleans and tied off and docked for a week. The crew kept busy doing repairs to the ship and wondering if tomorrow they would have a job. Captain Jack took the crew to town for supper and a meeting, everyone felt that it would an evening of bad news. With the river frozen, cargo would be very limited and the little cargo that was transported to lower states was not enough to keep the Packet boat operating.

His death was the beginning of a long journey

Captain Jack looked at his crew and commented "the news is not all that bad, everyone still has a job but things will have to change for a while, now enjoy your meal and we will talk later". That afternoon on the bridge of the Saint Mary, he explained that more than likely it would be three to four months before the Mississippi river was open to St Louis. There is not enough cargo to keep the Saint Mary profitable in the lower states, so until we can return we will be push barges in the Gulf of Mexico.

Jacob was heartbroken; it would be a very long time before he could be with Mary once again. Jacob sat down and wrote a long letter to Mary, explaining the length of time that they would be a part, he promise that one day he would make it up to her. The letter was received a few weeks later; Mary upon reading it grew sad. They both felt that without each other they were like a half a person. The time past slowly and every couple of days Mary would return to the levee and pray that the frozen river was once again free to flow.

The Saint Mary had to be unloaded of all unnecessary cargo and weight, a packet boat sets low in the water and in the gulf the waves were high at times. Captain Jack for the next few days explain the art of securing barges together, the Saint Mary's steering would be much more difficult and one little mistake would more than likely set the barges free. It would take days to catch and re-secure the runaway barges before the journey could resume and it would cut into the profit of the Saint Mary and any type of bonus the deck hands would receive.

The Saint Mary spent the next couple of days collecting barges, early the next morning the trip down the river began. Captain Jack believed that deck hands should be able to handle every duty on a packet boat and he had Jacob at the large wheel in the pilothouse that commanded the direction the Saint Mary would travel. Jacob was very nervous, true in the past he would relieve the pilot on long straight stretches on the river but the barges and twist in the river were another story.

His death was the beginning of a long journey

Captain Jack stood next to Jacob and barked out orders; he was like a nervous father watching his son performs a dangerous task for the first time. The journey to the gulf took most of the day and as the sun was setting the open waters of the gulf welcomed the new visitors.

The next morning as the sun was rising, for the first time in Jacob's life, land was not in site, just water and wave as far as the eyes could see. The waves were a few feet high and the Saint Mary rocked from side to side. Jacob felt ill, and had to discharge the contents of his stomach overboard, Captain Jack happen by during one of these discharges and slapped Jacob on the back. He commented "welcome to open water, son you are seasick and it will pass in time". It would be a few days later before Jacob received his sea legs.

In the open Gulf was the first time land was out of site, he asked one of the other crewmembers if the boat sinks which way do I swim. The crew member laugh and said, "if we are going, grab something that floats and swim starboard, if we are coming back swim port and soon or later you will find land". The trip took a little over a week and after a day on land a new load was ready for the return trip. This went on for a little over three months and in late May the Mississippi River was open to river traffic.

A load of cotton, coffee and goods were loaded and the trip began. The trip up the river this time was shocking, at some ports were packet boats that out stayed their welcome and the winter ice crushed their wooded skins and they lay deep in the water. Some were repaired to re-visit the waters of the mighty Mississippi River; others were sold off for equipment that they held and the wood that composed these great ships.

When the Saint Mary docked in Claryville for the first time Mary was not waiting at her usually spot. Jacob grew worried and thought maybe she just couldn't wait any longer and found another one to love.

His death was the beginning of a long journey

His thoughts traveled back to the past and remembered that Mary and his family lived less than a half a mile apart. They both worked hard at their chores and as the sun reached its peak and were half way to nightfall they would manage to meet somewhere in between. Mary was always the playful one; the path they took was always the same. More times than not, she would hide and wait for Jacob to pass, growl and grab him like a wild animal. Jacob would jump and sometimes tell Mary "I could have been a hunter and shot you dead because I thought I was being attacked by the wild bear that people are always talking about".

Sometimes he would be upset for a little while but Mary's smile and her deep blue eyes would make Jacob realize the love he held for her. Mary and Jacob were inseparable. Visitors to the area would always mistake them for brother and sister because they were so close. In Claryville it was always said that if you see one, the other one was not far behind.

The work on the river was the first time that they were apart for more than a few days. From time to time the Packet boat would stop in Claryville, to load or unload cargo; this would sometime take a few days. During these brief visits, he would spend it with Mary. He would beg her to wait, for one day they would have enough saved to have their own place to call home with fields of grain and corn, some chickens and a few cows.

To most it sounds very little but to Mary and Jacob it would be a future they could share. Mary stayed true to Jacob and many of the afternoons she would sit by the riverbank and wait and wish that Jacob would return home, if not for good, possibly for a few days or a few hours.

At night she would pray that Jacob would stay safe and that the next time she held Jacob in her arms it would be forever. Jacob sat on the stump where Mary was always waiting, and bowed his head down in silence. He sat for a little over an hour when he was grab and heard the sounds of a wild animal.

His death was the beginning of a long journey

It was Mary "the wild old bear got you again". Mary and Jacob hug each other for the longest time and tears were in their eyes. It was a long four months and each feared that the love for each other did not survive the time that they were a part. They spent the day together catching up for the time that they were apart. The time past swiftly and Jacob was gone once again.

The Saint Mary hauled a load of corn down south as they unloaded the cargo Jacob thoughts were with Mary. It had been four long years since he join the crew of the Saint Mary, just one more year and he could start his life with Mary, if Mary would have him. The Saint Mary was docked in New Orleans when Captain Jack called the crew together. "This trip up the river to St Louis will be the Saint Mary's final trip; we can no longer compete against the rail road". The railroads moved freight and produce at a loss just to drive the packet boats out of business. The crew grew sad and this trip up the river would seem the longest.

It was early spring; it had been a little over four very long years since Jacob took to the river. Mary had a spot on the levee where a large tree once stood; the stump made a perfect seat. Mary spent the afternoon after her chores were completed reading books, and wishing that Jacob would be on the next boat that docked. The ground around the stump was bare. The many afternoons she spent wore the ground down to mother earth.

She was enjoying the first warm day after a very harsh winter setting on the stump that the people nick named Mary's place but the sky was starting to cloud and it was beginning to drizzle a light mist. Mary started down the levee for her trip home; she glanced at the river. Far off she could see a curtain of rain traveling towards her, but there was a faint light, could it be the Saint Mary, could it be Jacob's Packet boat. Mary dreaded the rain, but something inside of her, something felt so right this time. Maybe the love that they shared for each other was a type of bond that the miles couldn't tear apart.

Mary for the first time knelt down and started to cry, her heart and very soul missed Jacob's smile, and his tender touch, Mary with her rain soak face turned to the heavens and pleaded with God to give her strength. The once beautiful smile left her face; her eyes were red with sorrow. She started her trip home not waiting for the Packet boat; she could not face another disappointment.

She was halfway through town when she felt a hand on each of her shoulders, and the words that were spoken were "the wild bear got you this time Mary". It was Jacob; they hugged for the longest time. Mary felt something was different this time, Jacob was not his normal self, he seemed very nervous. Jacob in the middle of Claryville knelt down in the mud and the rain and begged Mary to be his wife.

Mary was breathless and sad at the same time, she ask Jacob "how can we be man and wife when we only see each other a few times a year". Jacob just smiled "we have enough set aside to buy some land that we can call home". Jacob looked into Mary's eyes and said "Life will be hard at first but together we will make it, I love you Mary and I will never leave you again". "From time to time we will walk down to the river in the afternoons and wave at the boats as they pass because the river shall never separate us again".

Mary just smiled and asked Jacob if he would miss all the big fancy cities that he visited. Jacob looked down at his feet and said, "Mary I always hated being away from you. The only reason I worked on the river is so that we would have a good start. I can't give you the world I wish I could but we can have a nice home and my heart forever". Jacob looked up with tears in his eyes and said "I love you Mary please be my wife".

Mary at that moment made Jacob's dreams come true. They walked the rest of the way through town with smiles on their faces. It was finally over; the loneliness the deep aches in their hearts and the tears of unfilled love.

His death was the beginning of a long journey

MARY PAULINE

Mary grew up a short distance from Jacob; her family owned around two hundred acres of land. The land was passed down to Mary's father by her grandfather; this was common in the bottoms which made purchasing land a little difficult. Mary's father was named John Schroeder, John and his wife had one daughter and two sons before Mary graced this world. Her two older brothers help their father in the field; Mary and her sister Tina help their mother around the house. Rita was Mary's mother's name, and she kept them busy.

She had to teach her daughters the women duties on a farm that was not taught in school. In the spring they always planted a very large garden then in the fall almost a week was spent canning the produce. This process was long tedious, the jars and lids to store the produce in had to be washed and dried. A day would be spent collecting one type of vegetable; it would be washed, cooked and after it cool slightly placed in canning jars with the lids barely tight. Rita always took her time explaining each step as her mother did her. The jars were place in a canning pressure cooker, and heated. Rita explained to her daughters that if you do not watch the pressure on the cooker, it could explode, killing anyone in the room and blow the walls down.

Mary spent a great deal of time worrying and watching the pressure gauge, her mother laugh because she did the same thing when she was young. It took her years to trust a pressure cooker and know when everything came together and no one would get hurt. The following day was like the previous, pick another type of vegetable and the whole process would start all over again, this would go on for an entire week.

Mary in the mornings before breakfast had the job of feeding the chickens and collecting the eggs that they laid. Mary would always feed the chickens first before she collected the eggs; some hens were very protective over their eggs and pecked at the hands that were collecting them. After breakfast it was time for the pigs to be slopped, which was a term they use for feeding. Any food that was left from the previous day was mixed with grain and corn then dumped in the hog trough.

His death was the beginning of a long journey

The cows also had to be milked and turn out to pasture, most of the milk was served with the meals and some was turned into butter. This was one job that all the ladies would take turns at. The butter churn was a container that had a handle that had to be pulled up and pushed down; it took hours to make butter that would last the family for only a few days. The wash was always done on Friday, A large pot of butter beans and pork was placed on the stove and the fire was set very low. The water for the wash had to be heated by a fire, in a very large wash tub, then rinse, rung and placed on a clothing line for the sun to dry. By the afternoon when all the chores were completed the beans and pork would be ready to be served with bread made the previous day.

After supper and the dishes were washed, Mary would grab a book and head to the levee, set and read and wait for Jacob.

Mary looked up to her older sister Tina and wanted to be just like her when she grew up, she had nice cloths that was purchased new, but she looked forward to her sister hand me downs. She wore the same hand me down dress to church every Sunday. When she was younger and someone around her age made fun of her hand me down cloths, Mary's eyes would turn green with anger. If they knew what was coming next they would have ran, with her fist she taught them not to make the same mistake twice or at least with in her hearing distance. True she had a temper but she was also kind, to others and to animals.

When one of the farm animals became sick, she would hand feed them and kept them warm. She probably would have spent the night but her mother Rita would collect her wayward daughter and put her to bed. Mary would always end her day before she climb into bed, kneeling and saying a pray for all the good things in this world and for Jacob safe passage back into her arms.

His death was the beginning of a long journey

Jacob was on the river saving money to start their new life together, and Mary wanted to have a little money saved also. Some of the eggs that were laid in her parent's chicken coop she allowed them to become fertile and hatch. After one season the number of chickens double as did the number of eggs laid. Mary took the eggs to the general store and sold them at a very reasonable price.

She would spend the afternoons sweeping the floor in the general store; she posted a note in town that she was available to baby sit. Mary was a very busy person and late at night after her prayers she laid down very exhausted, wondering if she could continue another day. A smile would break across her face, and she would think about how much she loved Jacob and soon they would be together for the rest of their lives. In her dreams she and Jacob were one, never to part again. Every few days Mary would deposit money that she earned in the bank of Claryville, most time it would barely be a dollar but she knew it would build in time. On Sunday mornings Mary setting in the front row of the church, with Tina's hand me down dress, she would say a very special pray for Jacob to stay safe and for his return. The priest, father Moore would always smile when he seen Mary setting in the front row, and always comment our little angel is here it's time to start the mass.

MARY AND JACOB BECOME MAN AND WIFE

The wedding was to be held the following Month, in the small church of Claryville. The church held many fond memories; it was where they first met. It was during Sunday school, that Jacob remembered seeing his father embracing his mother and placed a long kiss upon her lips and he wanted to do the same because they seem so happy. He hugged Mary and tried to place a kiss upon her lips, Mary was surprised at first, and then she drew back and knocked Jacob to the floor. Upon hearing the commotion the Sunday school teacher entered and Jacob spent the next few hours setting in the corner. Jacob had the beginning of a nasty shiner and thought to himself that one day he would marry that girl.

It seems that Mary and Jacob plans were not quite the same. Jacob planed on spending the month find the land that he dreamed about owning and that could call home. Mary wanted a wedding that they would never forget, something they could cherish the rest of their lives. For the most part they went their separate ways.

Finding land for sale in the bottoms was not an easy task. The farms have been passed down from generation to generation. Jacob almost gave up hope until he heard about a piece of land owned by a gentleman in his early seventies with no family. The man's name was Jake and no one was quite sure what his last name was, about the only thing they knew was that at one time he was married to a lady that passed away a few years prior and they never had any children. His land was about 110 acres and hasn't been farmed for at least three years. Jacob decided to make friends with Jake and see if something could be worked out.

He purchased a bucket of beer and took a long a couple of mugs and headed towards what could be their new home. He found Jake setting on the front porch of what must have been a nice little home at one time. It was in dire need of repairs, to most it was a shack waiting to fall down, but to Jacob with some work it could be a nice little home, it was small but rooms could be added as time went by. Their parents lived just a few miles away, it would be a perfect place to live and raise a family.

He visited with Jake every couple of days and the conversation would travel between farming and the years Jacob spent on the river. They became fast friends or as they said in Claryville almost family. Jacob talked about trying to find land to farm and a place to raise a family.

He talked about Mary and their plans of marriage. Jake grew sad and started talking about his wife. They tried for many years to have children but God never blessed then with one. A couple of times she did become pregnant just to lose the baby half way through to a miscarriage. Jake patted Jacob on the back and commented that if I had a son I hoped he would be just like you. After a few more visits a deal was struck to purchase some farmland.

Between Jacob's pay and bonuses he managed to save close to thirty five hundred dollars. The going price of land was right at eighty-eight dollar an acre. Jacob read about a new piece of farm machine that was replacing the plow horses and it was called a tractor and they were selling for six hundred seventy five dollars. It would save Jacob a lot of work and he felt that he could make the farm more productive. Beside if this tractor worked as well as they said he could make some extra money plowing other people fields.

After a while Jacob had such a headache he just had to get away. It was a few day since he talked to Mary, He stopped by Mary's parent house to see her and it was the same story he just miss her. Mary and her mother were out planning something or across the river shopping in Chester. Jacob sat with Mary's father John and talked, at least he did, and John would just set and grunt every once and while.

After what seemed to be a lifetime for Jacob, Mary returned home, she packed a couple of sandwiches and invited Jacob to a picnic on the riverside of the levee. Jacob sat quietly and she did all the talking, after a while Mary sense something was wrong. She told Jacob that soon we will be man and wife, we will be together the rests of our lives, we must learn to face things together and not keep any secrets from each other.

Jacob talked about the cost of land, the cost of equipment to make the farm work, besides all that we will need money for seeds to plant and it will be a very long summer before the crops can be harvest and we will need money to live on. Maybe if I go back on the river a few more years that will give us the money we need to start our lives together. There was a long pause and Mary chinch her fist and grabbed Jacob by the collar," remember the first time we met, do I have to hit you to knock some sense into your head". Mary then smiled and said together we can make it work.

They went back to Mary's parent's house, she wrote down all cost of the land, the equipment and the money that they would need to live on. She wanted to work on it for a few days before they did anything else, and she commented to Jacob if she caught him by the packet boats she would have to give him the Sunday school treatment and her eyes turned green. Jacob all he could do

His death was the beginning of a long journey

was smile and remembered how much he loved this beautiful little wild cat.

Mary was not a shy person and when she put her mind to something, she was like a fox in the hen house. During those four years that they were apart she also manage to save money and had it in a saving account in the bank. The people in the bank were always happy when she came in. She would talk about her and Jacob's future, or about the chickens she was raising. Most of the things she would talk about were really not that interesting, but her eyes would always get wide and she had such a great smile that it would light up a room and people would enjoy the way she told her stories.

Mary would only deposit a small amount of money at a time, it was money she earned from selling fresh vegetables out of her garden, she also raise chickens and sold the eggs and the neighbors from time to time would need a baby sitter. Mary never found any job or chore too deeming and she was very frugal with her money, it was no surprise that she manage to save a little over five hundred dollars.

Mary talked to just about everybody in town, to try and find an answer to her and Jacob future plans. She even made a trip to old Jake and managed to lower the price per acre to fifty dollars. Jake wanted to keep at least ten-acres of land, because he would always say; "you never know what the future will hold". Mary's decided after talking to the man that ran the bank that they could get a loan that only required twenty five percent down, with the loan for the land, the equipment and seeds to plant. It would leave them with twenty two hundred eighty seven dollars and fifty cents in case the first couple of years did not go well.

Mary was proud of her self and could not wait to tell Jacob the good news. He was a little leery about borrowing money, but with those words he heard countless times, together we can, he agreed. Within a week, the loan was made and the tractor was ordered. Old Jake had more money than he had ever dream of having, and decided to travel the Mississippi river to see some of the sites in Jacob stories. It has been said that old Jake fell in love with New Orleans and started some type of business.

The wedding was still on track and Mary had just a few loose ends that she needed to handle. Many years prior her choice of wedding dress was already made. Rita Mary's mother saved her wedding dress in hopes that one day one of her daughters would choose to wear this wonderful gown that bought her so much happiness. A couple times a year Mary would beg her mother to see the dress and tell her all about her special day in church. She would ask her mother if she could wear that dress on her special day. Rita would laugh and tell Mary that she was saving it just for her.

The dress was a little big; Mary and her mother spent the afternoons altering the dress. They had time for long talks and Mary had many questions about married life. She wanted to be the perfect wife and Rita laughed because she went though the same thing when she was young.

She explained that no two women or men are alike. That Jacob has his ways and you have yours. That it might take many years or maybe a lifetime to learn to live with each other. Somewhere along the line you will both find a middle ground that will make your life happy together. Jacob seems like a good man but you will not know what type of man he is until you live together as man and wife. Things may not work out and maybe you and Jacob are not meant to live the rest of your lives together.

Rita went on to explain that there would always be a place for her at home. Her mother also talked about what a man and woman do behind closed doors when the children are asleep. Mary later that night thought about what her mother had said and laid awake and wondered if she was ready for her life together with Jacob. She said a little pray to God and asked for his guidance in making the right decision. It was a little past midnight when a broad smile broke across her face and she realized that she couldn't live her life without him, then she fell asleep and her dreams were of what was to come.

Mary stayed busy and the rest of the month went by quickly but for Jacob it seemed to take forever. Jacob arrived at the church early that morning of the big day. He was nervous and could not stand in one spot for very long period of time. When the Priest mentions that he left his sash to his robe in the little house behind the church, Jacob quickly volunteer to retrieve it. Father Moore just laughed and commented "son you are not going nowhere for a while".

The church slowly filled and when all the pews where full, town folks were forced to stand in the aisles and in the doorways of the small church. For many years the people of Claryville watched Mary and Jacob grow up together and to some, they loved the two as if they where their own children. No one wanted to miss this wedding, everyone in town knew that it would happen it was just a matter of time. Both

Mary and Jacob were bundles of nerves; they always looked forward to this day but never expected it to be in front of so many people. When Mary joined Jacob at the altar and they look into each other eyes, it was as if they were the only ones on this earth.

They felt each other's love and knew that this marriage was right.

When Mary and Jacob walk out of the church they tried to flee, they wanted to be alone. The people in the town, who were like family members had other plans on their minds and ushered them away.

Jacob and Mary were so busy planning for their future that they never notice that the people in this small town were also getting ready for the big day. The people of Claryville had planned a party for the new couple. Some of the town folks spent a few days cleaning out an old barn right outside of town and setting up makes shift tables. Some of the ladies in town spent the morning making different dishes, nothing fancy, just what the land could provide. Mary and Jacob were surprised and little embarrassed. Some of the men in town, when they had a few drinks of shine under their belts made a halfway decent band.

His death was the beginning of a long journey

The party lasted to the wee hours of the mornings but no one noticed or they acted like they didn't notice that Mary and Jacob were nowhere to be found. Mary and Jacob at the tender age of nineteen consummated their love. The times that they stayed true to each other made it even more special.

SOME TIME ALONE

Their honeymoon was spent in their new home, the first couple of days they just wanted to be with each other, they would take long walks through town and across their newly purchase farm land, holding hands and making plans for their future. It would be a few more weeks before the tractor would arrive.

Jacob spent the time repairing their new home and Mary spent the time cleaning the inside until they became lonely and one had to find the other. The two weeks pasted very quickly and the new tractor was waiting at the train station in Claryville. Jacob and Mary decide to start out early and make the three-mile walk into town and ride the tractor back. It was a little past eight am when they arrived at the train station and there was a crowd of people. Jacob's tractor was the first one in the area and the word spread quickly and ever one had to come and see this new fangled contraption.

His death was the beginning of a long journey

Most of the people consider it to be a waste of money and it would never replace the plow horse. Jacob found a quite spot and sat down and read the manual that came with the unit. After about an hour of reading he check the oil and gas and they were ready for the trip home. The follow day both Mary and Jacob took turns driving the tractor and plowing the fields, and then Mary returned to their home. She wanted to do some baking, house cleaning, she wanted to plan out a chicken coop for fresh eggs, and choose a spot for a garden,

Jacob plowed the fields, it took three times before the clumps of dirt were broken up and the roots of the weeds that called the farm home for a few years to be exposed to the dry air and to meet their maker. Jacob spent the next couple of week's plant corn. It was a slow process, he carried a stick to poke a hole in the earth, drop a kernel of corn then use his foot to push dirt over the seed, and this went on ever two feet.

Their day started before the sun rose and ended just before the sun set. Mary would make a lunch and would find Jacob somewhere in the field to have a picnic. At night when he returned home a hot meal would be waiting on the old wooden stove with some good warm rolls. Jacob and Mary after supper spent the time cleaning the kitchen so that they could spend more time with each other.

Some mornings, Mary would walk to the farm about a half a mile away to purchase or trade some eggs that her chickens laid for fresh milk. She would make these trips the day that the iceman would make his rounds in her area. Their icebox was made of wood with some insulation; a large door faced inside of the kitchen and at the rear was a smaller door that was on the outer wall of the house, so that the iceman could make his drop. Mary had to place a red card in the window to signal the iceman and place money in a jar that sat on the front porch to pay the man for the ice. The ice was transported by train form St Louis and would make many stops before it arrived in Claryville. The time of the day that ice was delivered was never the same and Mary always kept busy and didn't want to miss the drop.

His death was the beginning of a long journey

When the planting was completed, Jacob spent the time build Mary a small building for her chickens. He also had to repair the barn for the upcoming winter to store the tractor and some of the harvest that wasn't sold. Some of the corn would be planted next season, and some would be grounded up and make into chicken feed. Mary had names for all the chickens, and when one would quit laying her name was changed to supper.

Some of corn was picked early when it was soft and before the kernels turned hard and became live stock feed. When the corn started poking through the soil, Jacob walked the fields pulling weeds; the weeds would stunt the growth of the corn by taking away the moister and the nutrients.

During the time that he wasn't in the field, he built a pigpen and repaired an old smokehouse that was neglected for many years. Jacob would return home at night and look at Mary and comment that he was the luckiest man on this earth. One day when the rain came down very heavy and the fields were too wet to work, Jacob decided to take a day off. Mary was busy placing pots and pans on the floor of their home, Jacob was puzzled for a while until his notice that the roof had many leaks and she was doing the pots and pan thing to collect the rain water. "How long have we been having roof leaks" Mary commented that ever since they lived there and they would only occur when the rain was heavy and you were so busy I did not won't to bother you. Jacob spent the next couple of day's repairing the roof, and the next heavy rain they stayed high and dry.

THE FIRST YEAR

The summer past very quickly and the harvest was very profitable, and they both felt good that they were able to place a tidy sun into the bank. Mary's garden did well and she was able to can quite variety of vegetables. As summer turned into winter and the cold air took the place of the warm summer days. The chickens and pigs had to be place in the barn so that they could see another spring. One of the pigs was slaughter, dressed and cured in the smokehouse to make it last. The pig's head ended up in a large cooking pot to become hogs headcheese and a few mornings later, eggs, bacon and toast was served for breakfast.

As the bitter cold set in, they were kept busy stuffing rags in the outer walls to try and keep the house warm. Jacob promised that when the winter ended and the snow melted all the drafty spots would be repaired. Jacob would take one day out of the week and hunt for rabbits or maybe a deer to grace their table. Most of the time he never came home empty handed. Spring was always a welcome relief, their home would pick up strange smells from the candles and lamps they burned for light, the kitchen stove and the pot belly heater burned wood. It was nice to have the doors and windows open and get a little fresh air.

THEIR HOME IS TOO SMALL

The second spring in their new home, Mary was heavy with a child. It was mid May when the midwives were called and they were blessed with a daughter. Jacob insisted upon naming their daughter Pauline after her mother Mary Pauline. At first Mary resisted, then she realized it was a losing battle and little Pauline it was. Little Pauline by the time she was one year old, she had dark hair like her mother and she had Mary's blue eyes.

Many afternoons Jacob would return exhausted from working in the fields, but he would always found time to hold little Pauline on his lap and tell her stories. She was too young to understand but seem to find his voice very soothing. After a while little Pauline would asleep and Mary and Jacob would lie in bed and talk about each other's day.

It would be the spring of 1922 when the next addition to family would arrive and again it was a little girl and Jacob being bull head and still very much in love, pick Catherine Mary Gibbar as the child's name. Mary again tried to change his mind but finally gave up.

One night as they lay in bed, Mary grabbed Jacobs hand and apologized for not giving him a son. She felt that Jacob like many men wanted a son to help in the fields and carry on the family name. Jacob scolded her; "it was God's will that we have two daughters. If it meant for us to have a son, he would have given us one". "I love our children and all I care about is that they are happy and health". "I will love you Mary and our daughters until the end of time".

The daughters Catherine and Pauline just like their mother grew up to be tomboys, many days when Mary could not find them, all she had to do was take a trip to where Jacob was working and she would find her lost children. The children would mostly be under foot while Jacob was trying to work the fields but he did not mind. At night, he would get on his knees and thank God for his happy little family.

Mary and Jacob a few years later were blessed with a son. Mary by now was afraid of what name Jacob would pick. Jacob was surprised to have a little son this time and he was trying to think of a name, when Mary said it's my turn to pick a name. Jacob looked over at Mary and all he could do was smile and think of how much he loved this lady. Mary decide to name the son after her Grandfather, Clements and her lover and friend Jacob, the sons name was recorded as Clements Jacob Gibbar in the Claryville church records. The family now with five members grew too large for their small home; Jacob decided to add a few more rooms.

Claryville is located in the bottoms. One of the many problems that plagued the area is during the early spring the river rises and the water seeps under the levy and the ground becomes wet and soupy. Jacob decided to raise the land six inches under the new rooms that he was planning to build, and then move the family into those two rooms while he raised the old homestead the same height.

Between farming the land and rebuilding their home, Jacob found little time to sleep and he seemed to walk around in a daze most of the time. It was less than four months later when Mary, Jacob, and the kids stood back and admired their new home. Jacob fell upon his knee and asks Mary to marry him; Mary laughed, and felt a little embarrassed. Jacob look into her eyes and said "Mary I love you with all my heart and soul would you consent to be my wife" and Mary started crying out of happiness and said "yes I love you and I cannot and will not live without you".

Jacob grabbed Mary, carried her across the threshold, Jacob also made the kids wait until he carried each and every one of them into their new home. In the afternoon when things where quite Mary, Jacob and the kids would walk to the river and Jacob would tell them stories of his adventure as a deck hand on the old Mississippi river. Mary heard the stories many times but she would act as if it was the first time hearing them.

JACOB LEAVES MARY ONE LAST TIME

In the spring of 1927 as the river rose because of the snow melting in the northern states, the ground in Claryville started to turn to soup. Within a few days, the ground in some areas had about three inches of water. Jacob and Mary felt good that their home was high and dry. Some of the town folks of Claryville started to head for higher ground but Jacob wanted to wait for a couple more days because he felt the river would fall.

Claryville is located in the bend of the river and this time of the year the river moves very swiftly. The river started to eat into the ground below the levy; the river was creating something that the people in the bottoms feared the most, a sand boil. The sand boil dug a tunnel below the ground; it ran almost sixty feet before it burst to the surface. Part of the levee collapsed and the river started flooding this great little city called Claryville.

Jacob heard the bells at the church ringing and look toward the church, he could see the water rising and knew that part of the level had failed. He could see houses starting to float off their foundation, he screamed for Mary and the children and loaded them into a small boat that he used for fishing to take them to higher ground and safety. They were about a couple hundred feet from their home when the rest of the levy collapsed.

The swift water slammed the boat into a large object below the water line and little Catherine was thrown from the boat. Jacob jumped into the murky water and somehow manage to find little Catherine and placed her back in the boat. Then Jacob was gone, Mary looked around and spotted Jacob clinging to a tree a few hundred feet away. The swirling water was full of debris from

His death was the beginning of a long journey

the houses and homes that once made this small town. Mary and Jacob eyes met for one last time when part of a building or possible their home knock Jacob from his perch, never to be seen again.

It was a few months later when the water receded. The town folks returned to reclaim the few belongs that might have been left. Mary spent a few weeks trying to find Jacob but her search was in vain. It was as if the river reclaimed it lost child for a debt it felt that it was once owed.

Mary returned to their home in Claryville to find the place in shambles. With a lot of cleaning it could be a home again, the children were with their grandparents, the grandparents found a new home in Perryville. Mary sat down and cried; minutes ran into hours and into days. Mary just gave up on life, without Jacob, life had very little purpose. Sometimes late in the afternoon as boats passed the bend in the river where Claryville was once located; they could see a young woman setting on a stump by the old boat landing as if she was waiting for someone.

The last thing that Jacob remembered was something hitting him and the next thing he was floating toward a light in the sky. It was beautiful and Jacob started towards it like a moth to a candle but he did not feel whole. It was as if something was missing, it was Mary and the kids.

Jacob looked down and he could see them struggling in the small boat against the current and he knew that he could not help. He turned his head to the heavens and pleaded to God for help. Jacob's world turned dark, a lost soul to roam the earth possible to the end of time. Jacob tortured soul lost all track of time; the only thing that he did not lose was the love he had for Mary and their children. The memories stayed with him and it was possibly the only thing that prevented him from going mad. Jacob longed for Mary's embrace, a touch of her hand, if he could just look into her eyes just one more time. Jacob world grew cold and after a while he started to feel a weakness that he never felt before.

His death was the beginning of a long journey

Jacob felt that at last he would find peace, when suddenly a light from the heavens shone down upon him. It lighted the area and below he could see a body floating in a field of water. He felt somehow he was granted a second chance and that he would find Mary, he entered the body but he felt another presents. He felt that he was not alone and in a land that he was unfamiliar with. He was help out of the water and laid on the ground half in shock and total confused. It would take a few days for him to realize what had happen. Maybe he was drawn to this body because they shared the same family values or maybe God knew that this stranger would somehow help Jacob find peace and quiet and bring Jacob back to Mary and answer many of Jacob's questions about his children.

THE UNWILLING HOST

The unwilling host of Jacob's sprit or soul was a man named Robert (Bob) Wright. Bob grew up in a large city in Illinois called East Saint Louis. His mother's name was Kate, in her younger days she worked at a shoe factory in Perryville, through bad management and not keeping up with the times went out of business.

For a while Kate worked odd jobs around town and that was when she met Wayne Jenkins. Kate and Wayne love to party and after a brief affair, Kate found her self-heavy with a child. When Kate broke the news to Wayne, he treated her like a stranger. Wayne and his parents decided to move away from Perryville and leave their troubles behind. While Kate was carrying their child she met and married Bob's father, Bill.

Kate found out in a very short time that Bill was a mother's boy. Her mother in law was a very vindictive person. Kate tried everything to make peace with her but nothing ever seem to satisfy her. She found fault with everything that Kate did. Kate's life was becoming very difficult. During the second year of their marriage, Kate became pregnant and Bob was conceived. Kate and Bill started fighting almost daily; the mother in law was calling Kate a slut and that the child she was carrying probably belonged to another man. Bill was the fool, he was already raising another man's child and Kate is making a fool out of him again.

Bill never learned to stand up to his mother and gave Kate a choice of an abortion or raises the kid by herself. Kate was torn between trying to make the marriage work and the life that she carried. She spent a couple of sleepless nights trying to figure out what she should do. She decided that she could not and would not have the child aborted and that an abortion was murder. She knew that if she aborted this child she would have to face the guilt the rest of her life. She told Bill about her decision and Bill kicked her out. Kate turned to her family for help and they took her in.

Throughout my life I have escaped death many times.

I feel that God has a purpose or task that I must perform here on earth.

One day it will be revealed and my present on earth will be completed.

So that I can continue the journey into the light from the heavens above and to my love ones that wait.

Kate gave birth to Bob a few months later. Bill went to the hospital to see if the child bore any family resemblance. It took one look and he knew that Bob was his child. In Bill's family the males bore a birth defect, the birth defect was one or two extra

His death was the beginning of a long journey

fingers and Bob laid there with six fingers on his right hand. The birth defect was never discussed and while Bob was grown up he would joke that inbreeding probably caused it, by a couple of his ancestors.

Bob was trouble from the very first day that he was born. He was always getting into trouble or getting hurt. At the age of 9 months he was rush to the hospital floating somewhere between life and death.

He was with his mother in the back yard of the apartment that she lived in. One of the neighbors was cleaning tar off his old car with a mixture of gasoline and oil. He stored this mixture in a glass coke bottle and used an old red rag to apply and wipe off the tar. As he was working he placed the coke bottle on the ground, Bob loved the taste of coke and when he saw the bottle he stated to squirm in his mother arms and fussed. Kate after awhile decided to let Bob crawl around after all where could he go.

Bob crawled to the coke bottle and straddled it, before any one notice he took a drink. Kate look over just as Bob fell back wards and started turning blue. It was a mother's worse nightmare; watch one of her children die. They tried to make Bob vomit the gas, which only caused it to go in his lungs. Bob quit breath and as they rushed him to the hospital they tried to force air into his lungs. Everyone felt that it was a useless trip, that they were rushing a dead baby to the hospital.

Somewhere in the darkness a little soul floated away from his body, a soul that was free. Bob arrived at the hospital and the staff started pumping his stomach and forcing air into his lungs at the same time. They massage his tiny chest to try and get his heart to beat. The staff at the hospital worked a miracle that day and a tiny soul found his way back. Bob spent the next couple of days in the hospital and had many visitors, everyone wanted to see the baby that drank the gasoline and lived. This nightmare became etch in his mind for the rest of his life.

They say someone that comes back from the dead is blessed with a special gift and if this is true, then Bob's special gift was taking things apart and getting into trouble. After that episode He developed a great love for tools, he would set for most of the day playing with screwdrivers and wrenches. Kate though it was cute, what harm can it cause if he plays with tools. Toys cost money and they break easily and children become tired of toys in a very short time.

One afternoon when Kate left Bob in front of the television while she took a nap, Bob found his mothers pride and joy, her Singer sewing machine. Bob learned how to use his toys that day, by time Kate woke up; Bob had the machine completely torn apart. The machine was in so many pieces that it became trash for the junk man. Bob was banded from playing with tools for quite a few years after that.

When Bob was 6 years old he was enrolled into a catholic grade school that was about a mile away from his home. During recess on his second day he decided that school was not fun and decided to head for home. After recess, the nun sister Mary Philips took attendance and notice Bob was not in class. They made a sweep of the Schoolyard and Bob was nowhere to be found.

On the out skirts of the playground were railroad tracks that were heavily used and the nuns feared the worst. The police were called and the manhunt began. One of the officers went to where Bob lived and found him playing in the front yard and took him back to school. The nuns took out their frustration with a paddle on Bob's backside in front of the entire classroom. Bob decided that the next time he would not be caught and a few days later sneaked home again and hid in the house. It took his grandmother who was living with them, a while to find him. His grandmother wore out his backside; she loved Bob and was upset that he scared her so bad.

Bob might have been a very mischievous person but one thing his mother taught him was love of the family. Bob's birthday, which was November 22, and about every few years it would land on Thanksgiving Day. Bob loved this holiday; to him it was the most important day of the year because it brought the whole family together. He would see his grandparents, aunts, uncles, and cousins all together and thanking God for the feast that they were about to enjoy.

His death was the beginning of a long journey

When Bob was 7 years old and money was scarce, Bob thought this would be the year that they would all misses' thanksgiving because his mother could not afford the feast. He was happy that different family member gave him money for his birthday; Bob walked the 6 blocks to the grocery store and purchased the biggest turkey that his birthday money could buy. It was a comical site, a small child that barely weighted 50 pounds lugging home a turkey that was almost 15 pounds. He was very proud of himself when he presented the turkey to his mother. Kate carried on like it was the greatest thing in the world. That year different family members that knew Kate was having a hard time making ends meet gave her a turkey and after a couple of days she had three turkeys and no place to store the extra turkeys. Kate gave the extra ones away to less fortunate families.

Bob in his youth was very misguided, when he was in the second grade he thought he heard the calling to become a catholic priest when he grew up, but he was very impatient and decide to start early. He managed to secure some holy water from the church when no was looking and proceeded to baptize his fellow students on the front steps of the church. About a half a dozen were re-baptized before his little make believe church was closed by one of the nuns. The nuns were very harsh with their punishment, he lost all interest in becoming a priest and he became somewhat of recluse, his grades fell from the top of the class to barely passing. It would be many years before he set foot in a church again, but he carried in his heart the goodness that he could have done.

Bob when he was young was always on an adventure. True he may have grown up in a large city but he had a wild imagination and would create the adventures. When Bob was almost eight years old and after watching a war movie on television he turned to his mother and asked, "when I grow up will I have to fight in a war" Kate looked at him and commented that she didn't know. Bob spent the rest of the day thinking about the movie that he seen. It troubled him, most of it he did not understand except people suffered and died.

By the next morning Bob's thoughts of the war movie that he seen was a thing of the past. It was a brand new day and time for some new adventures. Bob was always getting hurt; sometimes it was through

His death was the beginning of a long journey

carelessness or maybe his lack of fear. Kate was always taking her son to the hospital or the doctor every time she turned around. His aunts and uncles would always say that if Bob makes it through his childhood alive it would be a miracle. Bob also had a hot temper and would get into fights at a drop of a hat. Some battles he would lose but he would win more than he lost. This went on for many years until one day when Bob was eight years old and his fight was with a girl. This girl was his sister, she was a few years older and always stood a full head taller over him and she enjoyed the almost daily beatings that she administered.

It was the fall of 1956 when like many other young men; Bob shot up like a weed and was a few inches taller than his sister. One day when they got on each other nerves and his sister decided it was time to teach Bob a lesson, the battle began but this time with far different results. The end came swift and with the defeat came her tears. The many years that she beat him up was forgotten, the sweet taste of victory was bitter. It was at that moment that Bob decided that he would never again raise his fist in anger. That he would try to resolve all future conflicts with words and only use fist as a last resort. As the years passed, Bob's battles became fewer; he walked away from many fights and felt the taut of his accusers. Bob never raised his fist in anger again.

When Bob was 10 years old there was massive construction project near his school. On the weekends when the construction site was closed, Bob and his friends would visit this area as if it was a brand new world to explore. They would play until the guards on duty spotted them and chase them off. The guards would make their rounds once an hour and they would always manage to spend the full hour or at least half of that in this New World before they were discovered.

The construction lasted over a year and almost every weekend they would sneak in until the guard chased them off. Towards the end, the site became boring and new places were found to explore. Bob's friend Jimmy decided one day to visit the construction site and tried to round up Bob and his friends but they found new places

His death was the beginning of a long journey

to explore. Jimmy decided to go it alone as Bob and his friends watched him walk away, they never realized that it would be the last time they would see him alive.

That afternoon when the guard made his rounds he found Jimmy floating face down in one of the many areas that held water. Bob blamed himself for not going with Jimmy to keep an eye on him. Maybe if he were with Jimmy, Jimmy would not have died. It was another cross for Bob to bear and from time to time he would think of Jimmy and always wonder if he could have made a difference. This thought hunted him for the rest of his life, maybe I could have made a different, and this was one of the reasons he volunteered to go to Vietnam. Maybe he can make the difference and save one life to pay the debt for letting Jimmy die alone.

On his fourteenth birthday Bob received a small shotgun as a present, it had seen better days but to him it was one of the greatest gifts ever. His mother was married many times and her current husband Don loved to hunt rabbits during the wintertime.

Don carried a large twelve-gauge shotgun that held three shells and if there was no chance of being caught by the game warden it held five. He was terrible shot and spent more on shells than the rabbits he brought home. Bob on the other hand, seemed like he was born with the weapon. He learned very quickly how to lead a rabbit and never found the need to use the site on the shotgun and shot from the hip. For the most part, Bob would bag his five rabbits and also Don's limit.

When Bob finally graduation from high school it was to the relief of his teachers that the problem student was gone. He started looking for employment but it was 1965 and the Vietnam War was at its height, President Johnson decided to greatly increase the number of American troops in that country. Bob's classification was 1A, which meant it was just a matter of time before he was called to duty. The good careers with a future were unionized, if he was able to secure one of these prized positions, then it would be waiting for him after his military duty was completed.

The story was always the same, he would be hired and one day before he could join the union he was laid off. It's rather sad to say but these young men, the future of our county, the ones that would lay their life on the line for the future of our country could not find decent employment.

The little time that he worked, he managed to purchase a car and pay his insurance for a year, his dreams of having his own place was put on hold. He lived with his parent and found part time employment moving furniture and drew unemployment. This would only last for a few months before there was a knock on the door and greets from Uncle Sam. Bob life was about to change for the worst and he would never be the same again.

His orders were to report to St Louis for a physical, if he were lucky he would fail and be able to secure a good job and a place he could call his own. During this time just about everyone was found fit to serve, about the only ones that failed were missing a body part. His basic train was in Fort Leonard wood and army life was really a shock, the men he trained with came from all sorts of backgrounds. One tried to rob a bank and was caught and was given the choice of prison or the service, couple of the others ones never seen a bar of soap and the smell was very over whelming. These were the people that Bob would have to live and train with for the next twelve weeks.

The time past slowly, the days always started out at five am, a drill sergeant running through the barracks screaming whatever words he found in the gutter, then it was fall out in front of the barracks. The drill sergeant walked down the line inspecting uniforms, missing button or if the button down portion didn't line up with the zipper on your pants then you were scream at for a few minutes followed by ten pushups. A mile run then to the mess hall for breakfast followed the morning routine.

The drill sergeant would control how much food a person would receive, overweight less food and the underweight more food than two people could handle. Then it was off for more training, Bob still didn't learn to keep his mouth shut and of course the drill sergeant from past experience learned how to deal with these types of problems. Hand to hand combat involved a chuck of wood to simulate a

His death was the beginning of a long journey

riffle with a little padding on both ends. Then you practiced beating each other up. The sergeant would pair each group, but for Bob he had to try and defend himself against four others. It didn't go so well but he did try to win a losing battle but it was hopeless. Every time Bob displeased the drill sergeant it was back to hand to hand combat. This went on quite a few times before Bob learned to keep his mouth shut and follow orders but deep down he was not defeated he just played along,

The riffle range was the part of the training that he enjoyed the most, second one was how to handle explosive. The twelve weeks of train passed slowly but it was finally over, and at the end was a one-week leave before the next duty station. Bob look up some of his old friends and a girl that he was very fond of. Bob just didn't fit in with his old friends and after swapping a few stories they went their separate ways. The girl that he was fond of was named Geri, they went on a few dates and promise to keep in touch and they did through the US mail. Over time they shared their deepest thoughts and desires, the love between them grew. To only be destroyed later by the war in Vietnam.

After a week of leave Bob reported to Fort Gordon George, for specialize training as a Radio Relay Carrier Attendant. His future would be setting up communication sites between base camps. In Vietnam he would spend his tour in a base camp which was almost like a ticket home without being killed or wounded. He had a knack for repair electronic equipment, as a teenage he rescued many electronic devices from neighbor's trash and repaired them and gave them away as gifts to his friends. He looked forward to the daily training; he felt that he finally found a place that was made to order. The twelve weeks of training passed quickly and he received orders for the next duty station.

He knew where he was heading without opening the orders, in basic training one of the many threats from the drill sergeant was "if you do not straighten up, I will make sure you go to Vietnam". It was a ploy to have trainees volunteer to go to war, and Bob grew tired of the threats and signed the papers for the war zone. He didn't realize that the decision would change his future plans forever, it would be something he

His death was the beginning of a long journey

would regret the rest of his life. When the orders were finally open it was what he feared,

In Vietnam he was assigned to the ninth division after a thirty day leave. He decided to make up for all the lost time that he was away and the follow year he would spend overseas. The first few days of his leave he was involved in bad automobile accident, he suffered bruises and cuts on his face, neck and arms, but not enough that he felt to put a damper on his 30 day leave. As he was waiting for the police to arrive he stood in the bitter cold air, he always ran around without a jacket and he stood there shivering in the cold wind, it was minus five degrees.

A few days later he begins to feel weak and started to run a fever. He visited the hospital at the local air force base and was diagnose with phenomena. He was given a couple of shots and some antibiotics. He tried to have his leave extended because of the illness but that failed. He made a date with Geri to make up for the time they would be apart, he mentions his orders for Vietnam and she grew very sad. The relationship ended with those few words,

Geri was afraid to continue a serious relationship with someone that would be in Vietnam in a few short weeks. He begged her to marry him, she looked into his eyes with a deep sorrow in her heart and she refused with tears running down her face. She talked about her two brothers that served in Vietnam, one was in a helicopter when it was shot down and the other died during a combat mission. The war had already taken two of her love ones away and she could not bear to lose another one.

She still wanted to be friends; they send letters to each other. The letters would continue for a little over six months, before they stopped. It would be a few more months until a he received the last letter, Geri became pregnant and married the father of her child after her mother made her move out of their home.

Bob reported for the flight to Vietnam, the stateside uniforms were traded in for jungle fatigues. A few days were spent at a military base in California, then late one night they were loaded onto a bus and shipped to the airport to board a plane for their new duty assignment. The flight was long and after twenty-three hours and a couple of refueling stops the plane landed in Vietnam. When the doors open, Bob felt the hot humid air of his new home hit him in the face. To him it smelt like death, the odor was unbearable.

Bob was assigned to a communications company, located at a base camp called BearCat. It was located in the southern portion of Vietnam, just 30 miles north of Saigon. Bob was assigned to Charley pontoon and after a few weeks was assigned to a communication site. The job was easy, the main task was to be at the communication site just in case something failed and failures were few and far in between.

Trouble was always one step away of trouble because of his nature. The site that he was assigned to was loaded with spare equipment. He adjusted a transmitter down to the lower FM band and connected it to a spare antenna then to a tape recorder. He built a radio station that had nothing but the latest and most popular music without the propaganda from the military.

The station had a range of about 50 miles. The word quickly spread and after a short time the station had more listeners then the Arms Service Network, but like all things in the military they felt that there was no place for this boot leg station that they had no control over. By now the station was on the air for almost 3 months when the orders were sent down from the higher ups to find and permanently take the station off the air and punish the ones responsible.

These make believe detectives were just a few minutes away from the radio station when a friend called and gave him the warning. He knew that this day would come sooner or later and had everything planed out, mentally he ran through the routine quite a few times in the past. The transmitter was never put together securely and it was easily broken apart and placed in the spare parts bend. The tape recorder was thrown behind a wall of sandbags and the upper part of the wall was easily pushed over and the recorder was buried under a couple hundred pounds of sandbags.

His death was the beginning of a long journey

By the time the officers arrived at his communications site, He was calmly reading a manual on the equipment that composed the site. The officers made a sound like they were clearing their throats; Bob acted surprised and jumped up and saluted the officers. He was question about the radio station that suddenly went off the air; He played stupid and after answering few more questions the officers left. The radio station was never to return to the air waves again, Bob felt he was extremely lucky this time and felt good that the station last as long as it did.

After a few more months' ninth division was reassigned to a new base camp called Dong Tam it was located south of Saigon. Bob was sent ten miles further and was assigned to a small communication site with 5th of the 60th infantry division. This was by far the easiest assignment. Bob and two others manned the communication site that linked this small outpost to the main base camp. Eight hour on and sixteen hours to kill, at a make shift library located in the chapel, He lost himself in the works of Jules Vern and after reading the full collection he started on Ian Fleming's, James Bond series.

The days and weeks past like a blur. The site had very few problems that were short lived and he moved up the ranks until he reached the rank of sergeant, along with the rank he was awarded a bronze star and an Army commendation medal. The rank meant very little but more pay and never pulling kitchen police agree with him.

He was reassigned to the main base camp and the next few days were spent on a haircut, polished boots and uniforms up to par, the transformation was incredible and he looked great. Being a sergeant, all you had to do was look good, take and give orders and keeps your nose clean and everybody left you alone.

Within a month Bob was assigned a communication site with four men under his charge. The site was to be the backup for the main communication site of 9th Division. To Bob it sounded very important and somewhat of a challenge. Something that he could lose himself in and help the time passes. Later Bob would realize the real reason for the site. The main communication site was hidden in bunkers and they wanted to draw fire away from it.

The men that were assigned to him were about the same age as Bob and some were younger, for the most part they were all trouble makes that nobody else wanted or trusted. Bob himself was a trouble maker at one time and felt with proper encouragement and training that he could turn them around.

The metal housing that the communication equipment was located in was in the bed of a very large truck. The housing had seen better days; the paint was peeling and had about twenty or more puncher wounds from rockets and mortars striking nearby. Some of the smaller holes were bullet wounds from snipers. The site was a decoy to draw fire away from the main communication site.

Bob and the men under his charge were expendable, the communication equipment was out dated but functional. It was a brilliant move by the officers and Bob would have to agree, if he and his men wasn't the target. The rockets and mortar attacks by now were creeping closer and closer at night to the main communication site. Bob and his men enjoyed not being the main target night after night, but that was soon to change.

The commanding officer sent a couple mechanics over from the motor pool to start working on the outer shell of the communication rig. After a few days all the holes were patched and a couple of coats of high gloss green paint cover the shell. Bob sat down and just shook his head he knew what was coming next. The rig was very visible from far away; to the enemy it looked like a very important target. That night a few hours after the sun set it began, the first mortar struck about 50 feet away. Bob and his men dove out of the site and started running, every time they heard another round flying through the air they dove in the dirt until it exploded and the routine would start all over again.

The journey to a bunker that afforded protection was less than five hundred feet away but to them it felt like it was a thousand miles. Between swimming in the dirt and running it took about three minutes

His death was the beginning of a long journey

to reach it but it felt like a lifetime.

After a few months of the same routine being repeated over and over at nighttime, the communication rig had more battle wounds in its shell than before. Despite all the short falls of the site and its location a department that Bob never knew existed, judged the site as the best in the ninth division. They would remotely check the quality of the communication channels for noise and log how many times the various sites failed and the amount of time it took for sites to be repaired and back on line. Bob's site was rated the best in all categories, and the men under his charged were awarded an army commendation metal and he was proud.

Bob's one-year tour ended in Vietnam and it was time to return stateside. But he had other plans; going back stateside was not one of them. Stateside twenty more months of army life was waiting. Twenty months of shinning boots, starch fatigues and doing mindless work to pass the days, weeks and months. The more Bob thought about it, the more Vietnam sounded better. If he could stick it out for eleven more months, the US Army would grant him an early out. Bob signed the papers to extend his tour another six months.

With the six month extension Bob, received a thirty day leave, all expenses paid from base camp to the front door of a place he called home. It didn't set well with his parents or love ones that he was returning to Vietnam after the leave. They counted the days for a whole year and each night said a pray that he would he would return home safe and sound and now the count was to started all over again.

The latter part of his tour he became pen pals with a young lady name Jane. She was from the same hometown as his mother and was very close friends with his cousin. She had two brother and two sisters. She was a small thing with almost black hair and green eyes. She stood at five foot and eight inches, she was a tomboy at heart and when she became upset or excited her eyes would turn blue.

Bob by now was twenty-one years of age and Jane was only seventeen. Her parents hated the age difference and Bob's hometown East Saint Louis was considered by most the wrong side of the tracks. The first time Bob met Jane in person was in a Nuns convent where she worked after school. Jane's parent didn't have a great deal of money but this was the way she earned money to buy cloths and pay for her lunches at school.

At first they were shy around each other, for months they exchange letters almost daily and sometimes the letters came two at a time. The letters were long and bore their deepest secrets but face to face they were speechless. Bob made

His death was the beginning of a long journey

a date with Jane at the only theater in town. The Mercers as it was called, it had only one screen and the movies most of the time were out dated but it would serve as their first date. They sat in the darkness watching an old movie called the Boston Strangler, when their hands met in the darkness and they felt each other warmth. Bob thoughts drifted from the movie screen and he remembered what type of person he had became.

He felt his life was turned inside out, he was not happy with the person that returned from Vietnam, He was not the same person that left. Jane was a sweet and innocent and Bob harden by the war and were returning to Vietnam. He remember the grief that Gerri felt when she lost her brothers, she was a change person that would never recover from her loss.

Bob felt that it was wrong to put Jane through the same grief. The time that they shared, Bob tried to gather enough courage to break the relationship off but after the third date it was too late. He was hopelessly in love and felt that Jane was one of the best things in his life and he would make it back. The thirty-day leave passed in a blink of the eye and it was time to return.

He returned to Vietnam to his old communications site and to the friends he left behind. After a few days everything fell back into place and as the days and weeks passed the daily letters spoke of the love, the loneness and the passion they shared. Jane would write letters about what was going on in her life, and Bob could not find the words that could fill half a page, there was too much death and destruction. He tried and create stories that made everything sound safe and sound but in the end they were not sent.

He found it easier to make up stories and create poems after a while Bob turned out to be quite a poet, he found it easier to fill the pages with poems instead of words that he found hard to find, he felt hollow inside. The personality that he left in Vietnam before the leave returned. The letters were filled with emotions that somehow were lost while serving in this country that was one step from hell. He lived a lie and it was eating him up alive.

The war in Vietnam was starting to unwind by now and division and troops were being re-deployed to Hawaii. Bob was given a choice of finishing his tour in the service in Hawaii or staying in Vietnam and try for his beloved early out. Bob thought about it for a couple of days, He thought about how Hawaii being state side duty would require him to follow rules and play by the rules in the worst way. Every time that Bob had to salute and officer it was like pulling teeth, he hated it and stateside would require a lot of saluting. Bob looked around and realized that Vietnam was not all that bad. If everything stays the same, the time would pass quickly and he could make it home early and in one piece.

Bob broke the news to his friends and commanding officer and they all thought he was crazy. Hawaii was still not home and there wouldn't be an early discharge. The division was in a hurry to meet the dead line for their departure. Instead of assigning Bob to another signal core he was assigned to an infantry group. The stay in the infantry group would be temporary until a more permanent assignment could be arranged.

In the infantry group due to his training he had an unauthorized MOS or job title to be sent into the field, which meant base camp duty until he was reassigned to another communication unit. Base camp duty, it lasted for couple of weeks until guilt set in, after a service was held for one of the falling infantrymen. Bob felt guilty setting safe and sound, and approached the commanding officer and almost demanded to join a squad in the field.

It was insane to give up the safety of the base camp, or it might have been a small voice in his head saying, "maybe I can make the difference". At first he was just part of the squad, but does to his rank of sergeant he became a squad leader. This title was a burden; he could no longer be the playful clown that kept him one step ahead of trouble.

A bad decision could mean someone's life; it was on one of these missions that the squad became careless; another member of the squad joined the point man. The point man's job was to spot landmines and booby traps. They walk side by side. They were busy talking about life; they were distracted and never realized that the area was booby trapped until one exploded. They were bloody but a live, the medic administered morphine shot to both of them and they were happy and felt no pain. All they kept saying was we get to go home now, we get to go home. The two were Medavac, and never to be seen again.

It nagged Bob, it was his duty to break up that twosome and he didn't, it was like a walk in the woods and every one became careless and two men were down. It was his duty to pick another point man, as he gather the squad, he could see the fear in each of their eyes. Who would he pick to be the next point man and possible send them to their death? He could not do it; he made a bad command decision. This squad had two sergeants, which was very rare; he bestrode the title of squad leader to the other sergeant and chose himself as the point man. If someone else is to be wounded or killed it will be me; I will not load another body onto a helicopter.

Bob was point man for land base mission, for the mission with the Navy be retained the title of squad leader. It was on one these missions that after a failed ambush, that he stood by the swift Boat counting squad members as they climb aboard. One of the privates wanted the task. Bob declined the offer and ordered him onto the boat. The private refused and after giving him the order the third time, Sergeant Wright locked a round in this M16 and gave him a choice, do as I say or take a round in the head. Bob felt this was a combat situation; lives could be lost standing in this open area. The private followed the orders and he swore to him self-that one day he would make him pay.

That day was not too far in the future, on one of the mission with the Navy. We were dropped off on a riverbank, on one side a rice paddy and the river at our backs. We set up as we did countless time before, side by side with a few feet between us, staring into the darkness, straining to hear any type of sound from the enemy. I heard someone whisper Sergeant Wright a couple of times. I started towards the voice, the piece of land that we sat upon was about six feet off the water and very narrow. Before reaching the sound of the voice the butt of a M16 struck the back of my neck; I fell face first into the rice paddy and was knock unconscious.

The private's revenge was short lived. I was help out of the water after what must have felt like a lifetime, half in shock and

His death was the beginning of a long journey

totally confused. It would be a couple more day for the full impact of what I experienced to be understood. As first fear set in, then grief, I wished I would have continued the journey to the light.

I felt something was different, I did not feel alone. At night my dreams were full of strange places and people, places that I never been and people I never met. My dreams were about a young woman, she had almost black hair and blue eyes, and she was holding a baby and two young girls stood beside her. For some strange reason, I felt a great love for her and the kids. My dreams would be about things we did as a family with this strange young lady and the kids. Was I going mad, I kept asking myself, who are these people that I never met? Why does it seem that it could be a page out of a history book, the cloths that they wore and the places that we visited? Was I going mad, who are these people, and where are these places that violated my dreams.

Bob felt that he was slowly going mad, he hated the enemy and could not wait for the next operation, an opportunity to get even. He carried extra clips for his M16, a couple of canteen pouches allowed him to carry fourteen grenades where the norm was only two. He looked forward to sandbag bunkers that they would encounter in the field; some of these bunkers were built by families to protect their love ones from bombs that were drop from the sky. But the taste of blood clouded his mind, and he made sure that they were destroyed and always hope that they would be filled with Vietcong. One day he found a D ring to place on his belt, the D ring allowed him to pull the pins on two grenades at the same time for more destruction. He was become a mad man that had no plans of returning stateside, if his life were to end it wouldn't be without a fight.

Jacob was an unwilling host to this madness and felt somehow that this must be hell. No way of leaving and no way of finding his way home. On one of the mission a blood trail was found, Bob thought maybe if he tasted the blood it would give him an ideal the age of the blood. Maybe it could give him an ideal how far the wounded Vietcong traveled, Jacob shared the taste of blood and if he could have vomited he would have.

His death was the beginning of a long journey

It was May of 1969 when Bob received word that his beloved grandmother past away, for the first time in months he found the strength to cry. It was his love for her that he again visited a church, on Sundays he would always stop and escort her to church; afterwards they would set around for the rest of the day talking and sharing a pot of coffee.

Bob was always interested in the stories she would tell about her youth. She grew up in Claryville and owned a farm; she would talk about her husband that he was very loving and a hard worker. The farm was about one hundred acres and they grew corn, raised chickens and had her own little garden. The story would always stop when tears came to her eyes; there was a sorrow that she just couldn't share.

Bob received an emergence leave to attend the funeral; he sat and felt sad that at the end of her life he was not there.

It would be a few more days before he was due to leave and time for one more mission with the Navy. The trip down the river didn't seem that long this time; his thoughts were filled with memories of his grandmother. The Swift boat's radar picked up a promising area and as the boat pulled in the Vietcong were waiting.

The night was filled with fire from automatic weapons, rockets and grenade launchers it almost seemed hopeless out gunned and out number, it's finally over. The swift boat crew threw the craft in reverse, everyone returned fire, and the swift boat 50-cal machine gun barrel started to melt. It almost seemed hopeless the explosion from the enemy rockets cause so much pain that it felt like a bullet or shrapnel ripping through our bodies, but each man stood back up and continue to return fire.

The swift boat managed to pull down river out of range of the enemy weapons. Bob walk around the boat checking for missing or wound men under his charge. All were accounted for, and by the grace of God no one was bleeding from a wound. There were bloody noses, cuts, bruises and soreness but everyone was accounted for and safe.

His death was the beginning of a long journey

The navy radioed base camp an within a few minutes the Cobra helicopters arrived and raking the area with rockets and mini guns firing two to six thousand rounds per minute. Within ten minutes the area was safe to reenter, the body count of the enemy was twenty-six confirmed kills. Weapons were collected and destroyed; the bodies were left laying for someone else to bury or to dry up in the sun.

The next day sergeant Wright was given the task of handing out Cong Badges, badges to wear on helmets or hats to let everyone know you took an enemy life for your country.

TOGETHER THEY FIND THEIR WAY BACK

Jacob found the strength to reach out and try to help Bob start his trip home with a memoir from long ago. His mind flashed back to a time when he sat in front of a television watching a war movie. He asked his mother if he would have to fight in a war and Kate commented "I don't know". His mind flashed back to thanksgivings he had with his extended families, a time of joy and happiness when everyone was laughing and enjoy being together. Bob look down at the Cong Badges and realize that each badge was some ones father or son. That there would be no happiness or joy in their household when it was time to spread joy.

His death was the beginning of a long journey

Sergeant Wright started crying and had to find a place to hide from the men under his charge, he could not afford to show weakness.

Bob's mind went blank and the next couple of weeks in the future would be a total lost. Later in his years after the tour in the service was completed he mention the sadness that he felt not being home for his grandmother funeral.

His sister looked at Bob puzzled and commented "you were there". You acted strange like you were another person, we didn't know if you were going crazy with grief or what. You spent one day in the bottoms digging holes in this farmer's field until you found a body. It was strange, it was just a skeleton and with it was a rubber pouch with a wallet, the name on some of paper were hard to read but it was our grandfather Jacob Clements Gibbar that died back in the twenties. You smiled and they heard you say "Mary I am coming home" or something like that, and then you ran to the old levee across from Chester and passed out. You spent the last couple of days walking around as if you were in a cloud. We were worried and felt maybe a couple of days of rest may help and before we knew it you were gone.

We received a letter a week later express sadness that you miss our Grandmother Mary Pauline Gibbar funeral. You wrote her name quite a few times and your letters were just not the same after that.

Jacob found strength in Sergeant Wright's moment of weakness and for the first time taken control of the shell that they shared. The letter that Bob received mentions the death of Mary Pauline Gibbar and he felt that it must be my Mary. Somehow, someway God was sending him home, he remember his last moment on this earth and how he died a few feet away from a tree that was barely large enough to be consider a tree. Mary and Jacob planted that tree a few days after they became man and wife. His memories were as clear as the day the levee broke and he lost sight of his family. Jacob ran across the new levee and he could see this lady standing on the old

His death was the beginning of a long journey

levee as if she was waiting for a boat to arrive.

She was rather slim, she had black hair, and she was dress in cloths that appeared to be outdated. She was so occupied looking down river, she never notice someone sneaking up behind her. She felt a hand on each of her shoulders and a voice that melted her heart "the wild bear got you this time Mary". Bob passed out and once again his body only held one soul. Mary and Jacob walk down the levee smiling and as they look into each other eye Mary said, "If you ever leave me again, I will give you the Sunday school treatment"

Bob after his military duty was completed would find out later his mother was from Claryville and moved to Perryville after the great flood. He knew her as Kate but as she explained everyone in Claryville had nicknames. They somehow came up with a nickname of Kate but my given name is Pauline Mary Gibbar, your aunt's name was Catherine Mary and your uncle name was picked by my mom, she named him after her grandfather and my father.

Clements Jacob Gibbar, but then she had a question, what made you dig up that farmer's field, how did you know my father would be there?

Bob smiled and said "I was a lost soul in Vietnam with no plans on coming home alive, somehow my grandfather help me see the errors of my way and helped me find my way home." He then sat down and shared the memories that he and Jacob shared for the last six months. He told her about the adventures on the packet boats in the very early twenties. How in New Orleans Jacob purchased a rubber pouch to keep his wallet dry, He share other memories that Jacob share with him and Kate after a while had tears in her eyes, she never knew of the great love that her parents shared.

Somewhere in the heavens Jacob and Mary stared down, and were very proud of how their children turned out. That night as Bob slept he had two visitors, Mary and Jacob returned and gave their grandson a huge and thank him for helping them find their way home and into each other's arms.

His death was the beginning of a long journey

It was a few weeks before thanksgiving, and Bob thought this one would be very special. He started making bread; he didn't measure anything, just a pinch of this and a hand full of that. That afternoon a couple of his family members commented that it just like your grandmother's bread maybe a little better. Bob smiled and said no one can make bread better than Grandmother Mary Pauline Gibbar, a friend that I owe my life to, taught me how to make this bread. It was an art form that was passed down from his grandmother from Germany many years ago.

The end

ABOUT THE AUTHOR

Bob grew up in a town in Illinois; His family came from a little town in Missouri called Claryville. He served two tours in Vietnam and after his military duty was completed, he married his pen pal Jane and moved to New Orleans. Hurricane Katrina destroyed their home and they found a new home in Perryville, MO. Perryville is located about twenty miles from Claryville.

Made in the USA
Columbia, SC
24 January 2023

10954895R00065